Begin with the End in Mind

Begin with the End in Mind

Emma Healey

Arbeiter Ring Publishing, Winnipeg

Copyright ©2012 Emma Healey
Arbeiter Ring Publishing
201E-121 Osborne Street
Winnipeg, Manitoba
Canada R3L 1Y4
www.arbeiterring.com

Printed in Canada by Coach House Printing
Cover image by Jeanette Johns
Design by Relish New Brand Experience Inc.

With assistance of the Manitoba Arts Council/Conseil des Arts du Manitoba.

We acknowledge the support of the Canada Council for our publishing program.

ARP acknowledges the financial support to our publishing activities of the
Manitoba Arts Council/Conseil des Arts du Manitoba, Manitoba Culture, Heritage
and Tourism, and the Government of Canada through the Canada Book Fund.

Arbeiter Ring Publishing acknowledges the support of the Province of Manitoba
through the Book Publishing Tax Credit and the Book Publisher Marketing
Assistance Program.

Printed on paper with 50% PCW.

LIBRARY AND ARCHIVES CANADA CATALOGUING IN PUBLICATION

Healey, Emma, 1991-
    Begin with the end in mind / Emma Healey.

Poems.
Issued also in electronic format.
ISBN 978-1-894037-62-4

    I. Title.

For Alison, Michael and Moira.

The citizens in their cars looked at the porcupines, thinking: What is wonderful? Are these porcupines wonderful? Are they significant? Are they what I need? — DONALD BARTHELME

TABLE OF CONTENTS

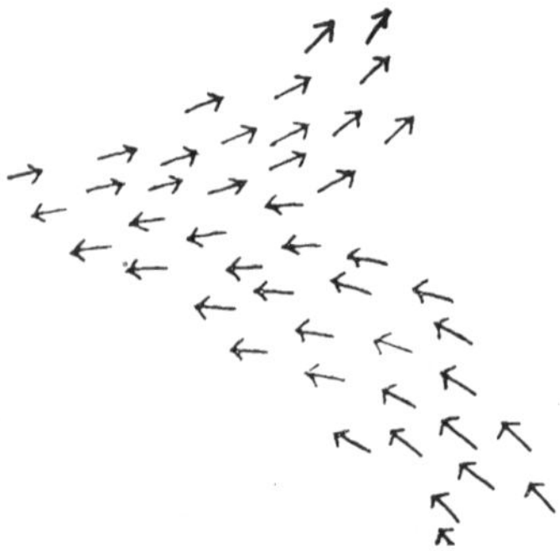

Everything Is Glass

My full name is Emma Flannery Lawrence Healey. There's
a reason. I tell this story a lot. My mother went into
labour with me during a screening of *Edward Scissorhands*
in Toronto, January of 1991. It was snowing. They didn't
own a car. You don't need to know this: the light on her
face or the speed of her stomach and hands, what my father
said, how they stayed for the whole thing anyway, how the
snow, how the sound. On my kitchen floor now where
I'm sitting to write this, there's a half-empty carton of
ruby red grapefruit juice, pulp-free, and a cookbook titled
Becoming Vegetarian which I'm not. What I tell people isn't
exactly like this, what I'm telling you here. I own seventeen
T-shirts and twenty-five pairs of socks. I counted, just
now, for this. My left foot is bigger than my right by two
millimeters and I'm blind in one eye. 5'6"ish, Earl Grey
tea always with milk and sugar both these things are about
me. How about this: My mother went into labour with
me in Vancouver, September of 1989, the same day the
Monkees disbanded. My father was changing a lightbulb
in the living room and broke it when he heard her scream.
Glass everywhere, and even with her going Michael I
think we have to from the kitchen face-up on the freezing
linoleum he just stood there barefoot and both eyes on the
shine of it. They did not own a broom. It wasn't raining.
Twenty-two pairs of socks and three pairs of tights I guess

is more accurate, and orange pekoe sometimes. It's my
right eye the blue one and I don't mind, I can see through
walls. I like orange juice better than grapefruit. When
I was born, '92 in the Peterborough General Hospital
mid-August, my father who didn't know this was going to
happen picked pieces of glass from the treads of his shoes
and thumbed through *Today's Parent* magazine, the nurses
somewhat surreal at Peterborough General, all male for
some reason and wearing scrubs exactly one size too small
each, uniformly, all of them, due to some clerical/ordering
error, my mother different-roomed glossy with morphine
still awake and breathing like traffic. My kitchen floor now:
three half-empty bottles of white wine, one full grapefruit,
four lightbulbs, a breadknife, three pairs of tights, *A Good
Man Is Hard to Find* or *Brief Interviews with Hideous Men*
or a cookbook two T-shirts a measuring tape and a sock.
In the bright white of the credits and gasping my mother
coat half-on and no shoes said to my dad I think Emma
and he said No I think Flannery. I don't actually own a
measuring tape, I was exaggerating, I'm sorry. I have one
of those elementary school thin plastic rulers that's thirty
inches long and I climbed the thing up my side and marked
every end point with red pen, which is why 5'6"*ish*. My
left eye is pretty bad too but that's not the same thing, the
hospital strangely quiet and poorly lit my mother with

arms crossed over her swollen stomach and hurting my
father made arguments: morals, peafowl, Southern Gothic,
and my mother said Kissed once only once and my father
said Lupus, because of the lupus and she said Exactly,
what's wrong with you which is how in Cobourg, Ontario
in August of '90 I started my first ever argument about
Death of the Author, my father still covered in glass and
my mother still breathing. A male nurse in what looked
like shorts poked his head in to see if everything was okay.
My kitchen floor's covered with lightbulbs and books now,
so I'm sitting in the sink with my laptop balanced on my
knees. I have tights on. My mother said I'll arm wrestle
you and my father said What and the nurse said Okay and
nobody thought about *Edward Scissorhands* because that
movie still hadn't come out yet. The paradox here is that
if I get up then I'll step on the lightbulbs and ruin these
tights so I'll have to rewrite it, this whole thing, it has to
be true with both of their faces the hospital still wet and
shining with weather it happened the floor and my kitchen
the thing with my mother and father, I tell this a lot. My
father said yes and my mother said nothing, and neither
with breathing and sharply let anyone win. Which is why
I'm here now, and in tights and with glass in the soles of my
shoes and my hands and I'm telling you this, and it's true.
There's a reason.

Things Have a Mind of Their Own

and that's just how the world is. You can't fight it; leave
one cup in a cabinet overnight and it grows roots blooms
stacks of juice glasses, starts menacing the hemispherical
bowls out of their real estate. The kitchen sink catching
sight of your hands whispers No, your bookshelf re-
alphabetizes itself and by author not title and era the
way that you like it. You eat pad thai for breakfast out of
a coffee mug and necessity. When you open the door to
your closet all your shirts sing the national anthem off-key.
Things close themselves and open and have souls without
your permission, and the phrase I Live Alone is more
slogan than statement of fact because really you live with
concurrence and later you find the bowls of course they're
under an armchair and dusty as fuck so you leave them and
stumble downstairs in the wrong clothes singing quietly
and sometimes the bus is right there at the corner and
waiting and maybe today it's a bus or it's maybe a caterpillar
but either way you dig for your wallet the world swells and

For My Neighbour

I'm alive and it's spring so of course I had to break into
someone's apartment. Your kitchen smells like cinnamon
but you don't actually have any cinnamon anywhere, even
in the pantry, I checked, which is strange and I'm sorry.
I didn't take anything almost. There's a hole in my shirt
where it caught on some glass or some wood I'm not
worried about it, I duct-taped the frame back in place
plus the edges. Your fridge is ill-stocked and there's no
better word than *osmosis* for this I don't think. I brought
the *Penguin Dictionary of Literary Terms and Literary Theory*
with me, it's heavy and corners just dying to meet some
poor eyelid or wrist and standing on your balcony I ate the
entry for Free Association without reading it first. Which
action I am now regretting slightly. My elbows feel stuck
through with thumbtacks and you have a mediocre DVD
collection and I cleaned your bathroom sink just a little
because why not now I'm here? What I mean is, our walls
are thin, and how you sound is how I get to sleep. Your
girlfriend has boots and a laugh so loud and high that my
radiator rings out chords against the wall when you kiss her
and every night around 11 you wash the dishes or practice
the harmonica, I can't tell. You have cats or else parents,
either way there's pacing. The *Penguin Dictionary of Literary
Terms and Literary Theory*, whose title I originally misread,
made a symphony free-associating with your front window

most of which I cleaned up and your bedroom wall tastes
almost exactly the same as mine. There's linguistics stuck
somewhere in this, I'm pretty sure. If you hear me land,
drunk and singing and shoes-on in bed around dawnish
that's discourse. I took your left slipper to prove this.
We have the same placemats. I'm not sure what else I
should tell you.

Not Good Enough

I phone this song at 8 a.m. and after two rings it picks up
but doesn't say hi. "Hi," I say, into the silence. This song
and I have been best friends since the seventh grade and it
knows why I'm calling. It knows everything. Have you ever
had a best friend? This song and I do everything together,
we finish each other's sentences, we have nicknames for
people we don't like, I can call it whenever. Sometimes
things get so close it's like sharing a spinal cord. We
breathe the same. We repeat ourselves. We get each other.
This song and me. "I'm heartbroken," I say anyway. My ribs
swell and ache when I breathe in. I can hear it lighting a
cigarette. "Like but actually though." This is true. Things
are not good. I'm sitting on the kitchen floor wearing
men's boxers and a dumb T-shirt, with my knees pulled up
to my chest. So far tonight I've eaten three toaster waffles,
all dry, two still frozen a bit in the middle, and half a thing
of "Italian-Style Seasoning" because it was green and in the
cupboard and I don't know. You know how in CPR training
they tell you that to save someone who's not breathing you
have to crack their sternum first? This song knows I hate
silence. Even though we're exactly the same height people
always seem to think it's taller than me. I can hear it exhale,
long. I wish it would say something. "I'm going to go to the
clinic. I feel like I'm going to die." Quiet, still. I spent all
night pacing around, remembering things, and my hands

won't stop shaking. The kitchen floor suddenly seems like the wrong place to be, I can feel morning starting to push through the windows like it's going to climb over me. "I looked it up on WebMD. It's a thing." The silence goes, Heartbreak? I'm blushing now, into my knees. I can picture it lying in bed, dangling its non-phone hand lazily over the side, smoke listing up, with the hedgehog skittering in nervous spirals on the hardwood like it does. I've never seen this song sleep. I'm not sure if anyone has. My breathing is weird-paced and ragged. My arms feel too hot. I go, "I can't deal with this anymore." I go, "What I'm saying is." What. Still the silence. I've been awake for a full day, I feel flushed and bruised and stupid for calling. Can somebody explain why me and this song are still friends? When we go to parties everyone always talks to it first even though I'm clearly the better conversationalist, and last week it invited me out to the movies and then never showed up or said sorry. This song answers its texts maybe 30% of the time and never asks how I am and when we were seventeen it would steal my little brother's Adderall and sell it to kids at the Catholic high school across the street, like I wasn't going to notice, two weeks ago it borrowed my favourite pair of jeans and has yet to return them and probably it never will, probably it's wearing them right now, lying there in bed, not listening to me, this song has a stupid haircut. I don't care.

"Are you sitting on your kitchen floor wearing men's boxers and a dumb T-shirt?" it asks.

"No." Whatever.

"Okay."

I've been eating my food out of mugs because doing the dishes is too much for me, because of the breadth and intensity of the heartbreak I've been feeling, and how hard things have been, how I haven't been sleeping how everything tastes like pavement anyway except now there aren't any left so last night I made tea in a salad bowl and just drank it that way, tipping the side of the bowl to my face, on the kitchen floor. I can hear this song smiling, down the line. One time at a party it stole some guy's wallet just because he'd been mean to me and we bought three 24s of expensive beer with his credit card and then threw all his I.D. into the river. There's sun now and I can sense my roommates moving, through the floorboards. I feel tired for the first time in days maybe. Bird-sounds. Something diffuse in my bloodstream. This song doesn't say, but I know that it's lying there, grinning its stupid smug grin with its eyes closed, just waiting.

Expedition

you don't ever go back there this for a reason all the forks
ever unopened bank statements flyers for night foods the
sad edge of an excellent lemon curd coils turns toward you
and lowing the filthy tall green of your centralest metaphor
posturing upward except for when you pull it's not filament
drainage or slight but a whole bench-pressed hockey team
lazy with silverware long squinting into your curtainless
sorry head down and dig back a signified not sorry just
more plug everything in ever straighten once hums with
a new sense of push it in chorus they large with your
shoulders push out

Begin with the End in Mind

On Sunday of last week I saw on the subway a boy who was
reading a book. On the subway from low plastic seating
I saw he was holding it, facing the doors where the exit
was, studying slow as we pulled into some middle station.
The secondmost lesson you learn in this book is that all
things create themselves twice. I know this from Google;
I looked it up later, at home, with the screen and my face
glowing twice a bright blue. I did not know this yet, on the
subway. Last Sunday the plan was to go to the gym and
then grocery store and then home. I'd done two. We got
stopped in a tunnel. The speakers all crackled. It sounded
like sea. I had beans in a bag, from the grocery store, and
some milk, and my legs hurt, a little. The primary part
of the secondmost lesson you learn on the subway from
reading this boy and his book is that first, things get made
in your mind. The boy knew this already I'm sure. His page
number looked sixty-fiveish, at least. Consensus is first that
you think about something, then your something gets set
into motion. When I sit at my desk with the silver-edged
screen and my skin all lit up I don't think about anything,
usually. The website I found for this book had these
concepts like Conscience and Self-Aware Living all listed,
with bullet points. When the boy found a word that he
liked he would swish up his eyebrows like blinds that you
pull with a drawstring. He was wearing a scarf. When the

lights in the subway went out I got nervous. I always get
nervous when things don't conceptualize. The boy kept his
eyes on the book. The air in the subway was ringing and
pitch-gray. When I shifted my weight on the low seat my
plastic bags rustled like static from speakers in ceiling. The
boy started following words with his fingers and mouthing
them, Braille-like. We start ourselves now, in this moment
or tunnel, slow, homebound in darkness, the book says,
and rustling. We start something simply by shedding
our scarves and thinking the end of things hard as we can.
Call it sea change. Last Sunday was when I had not yet
gone home so this hadn't yet really like crystallized. So
instead I just sat and looked up and heard sounds coming
tinny through everyone's headphones, cacophonous
stillness. And then someone fixed it, like that, which is
how things get fixed and which always surprises me, always.
All the lights switched themselves and I shifted and he
swished a page and we all with our gravity started on
homebound, with nothing but end in our minds.

Indigo

if I could hire a team to re-order, -label, and -stock my
nervous system every twelve hours I'd do it absolutely
wouldn't you yes amazing to not seize amazing the huge
walls the swallowing petty theft slow golden ratio glottal
the staircase unfolding all lazy spring grow-your-own
trees from a kit just to slip you come new season early
under nothing has ever been wet here nothing will be I
do not like nature but I do like to be one coherent linear
system in the fluorescent diffuse small of a larger complex
million individual discrete systems all better indexed more
reasoned about love and mystery and reference etc. than I
am there's no much that's too slow to swallow the volume
a tree graph a whole poem stands you can close for it only
in light of your reference a sprawling nonfiction is this
glorious beautiful compounded

Heritage Moments

There are many things in this world which you may already know and love—bonspiels, alacrity, insulin, Ryan Gosling—but **were you aware** that most of these things are Canadian?

Canada has produced many great works of art and also much weather. Despite this, many people are still sadly ignorant of its finer points—its multiple residents, its interior design. Canadians have been variously described; some own guitars and if you like you may kiss us. What you have heard about our politeness is true but it is a nuanced and delicate social apparatus and not to be taken lightly; we are tense and relieved like bad music and publicly, often. Wistfulness and pilsner are inherent. Winter is a learned behaviour.

Did You Know?

· Canada's official national sport is ice wine.

Canada is often the second-largest country in the world, and one of the least densely populated. The country's most valuable export is distance, which we ship mostly in crates overseas to less fortunate countries, and sell at a premium.

As with most populous land masses, our country's physical boundaries—coastlines, etc.—enclose or expand to fit our people. Widely accepted geological theories of the 19th and 20th centuries held that there was a direct correlation between the number of citizens in a given country and its overall size—that place functioned, in some way, according to us. We of course know now this is far from the case.

At present, if you spaced all Canadian citizens evenly across the country there would only be 1.5 people per 16 square km. of land, which is one of the reasons why we do not do it.

· Canada's smallest recorded year was 1982.

Canadian history is famously heartbreaking—so much so, in fact, that until the late 1980s it was illegal to teach in public schools. Before this, the only sadness ever glimpsed by our children was in counterfeit, a dim outline; kids swapped copies of the Charter for snack foods, young boys hid old volumes of Hansard under their mattresses, Sir John A. MacDonald's astringent ghost lingered on the borders of our nation's playgrounds, waiting to pick off the weak ones. The true burdens of our past—its loneliness, its endless woods, its weeping—once resided only in the hearts of those old enough to drink or fly aircraft. Debate over this issue continues to this day.

- If you say the word "Notwithstanding" to any Canadian citizen, they are required by federal law to spin around three times, give you any cash they may have on their person, kiss your left hand, and back away slowly.

The border between Canada and the United States is the longest unbroken physical border in the world, much to the discomfort of American politicians, urban planners, etc. Imagine you meet someone, take them home, promise to call the next day when they ask you, and then never do; feel a minor guilt, and then forget about it. Imagine the next time you see this person, centuries later, the two of you are trapped together in a stuck elevator, unlit, and zip-tied at the legs. Several states have made halfhearted attempts at receding, but their shame, and our geological inability to let go, have prevailed. The Canada-US border is extremely visible from space; it resembles most closely an endless, humiliated tangle of fluorescent tubing.

- Our passenger rail system is named after a preposition, though we do not think about this too much and neither should you.

Louis Riel's diaries describe one bleak winter when Canada stopped returning his calls.

Though they had their differences, the notoriously co-dependent Riel could not bear the thought of having to exist without the country he had spent his life fighting for. Less than twenty-four hours after his first unanswered message, Riel began amassing search parties, designing posters, rending his garments and weeping bitterly into the Red River.

Besides his closest friends, few participated in the first week of the search—in truth, most of the citizens of Canada paid little attention to the situation, or to Louis himself, who after a week had taken to wandering the land in complete disarray, moaning low vowels into the dry prairie air. However, as time passed, concern began to spread across Confederation. People grew restless: snow was held, shops closed, women were whispering prayers into the sewer grates and men phoned their ex-lovers "just to see how [they were] doing." Riel himself was distraught beyond recognition, and his mustache grew heavy and wide with sadness.

(It is important to remember that at this time, Canada was still a new country; its people were not yet ready to be unsettled.)

Ultimately it was a young *coureur des bois* (French for "Boy Runner") who discovered Canada again, six months to the day after Riel's initial search had begun, by breaking into the front window of its apartment using only a fire escape and a credit card. Upon climbing into its living room, the young man discovered the country sitting cross-legged on its own couch, gazing affectionately into a half-empty bottle of rye. Canada was heavily bearded but otherwise unharmed. The *coureur*'s own account of the event describes the look on the country's face as he moved toward it to take its hand and guide it back outside — to a flushed and glassy-eyed Riel, to the cold, to a citizenry who already, you could tell by the sound, were thronging the streets with relief — thus:

Wryly amused; possibly irritated.

This phrase is now printed on all our official currency and letterhead. The occasion itself is marked with a holiday known as "Canadian Thanksgiving."

- Contrary to popular belief, there is no such thing as a Canada goose. All geese are, in fact, inherently Canadian, and also lined with tiny magnets to facilitate North-South migration.

Our national anthem, "O Canada," was composed by Calixa Lavallée in 1880 and consists of an extremely elegant hand-drawn map which at present is reproduced in countless textbooks as well as on the walls of most government offices. Traditionally, students and young children are required to stare at the map for 1–2 hours each day, usually in the mornings, until the image has impressed itself thoroughly not only on their retinas but on their conscious and unconscious minds, until their nerves, when they ring, ring provincial. In this way is insured a national impulse where all gestures, regardless of content, represent an act of communication between Canada and gesturer, where there is new semaphore even in sleeping or touching or shopping or talking; x-ray any of us and it looks like a misfiring atlas. The commission of sympathy—unconsciously federal, immediate—is at the core of all things. With Canadians there is always the question of staying; the act, once again, of deciding to stay.

There is also an alternate version of the anthem in French.

Spring Line

The sea as they say is upon us. It's summer. There's little to
hope for. It has already taken our bedsheets, our power and
parents as we're sure it will one day take us. Without guile.
We're not waiting. There just isn't much left at this point—
we can swill, wreck ourselves on the hardwood, send some
practice flares up through the lesser vents, but none of
it cures the malaise, strains the salt from the cheap beer.
Those among us who know how to fix it have long fled to
elsewhere—to Dawson or Guelph, to superior bodies of
water, ones that don't leave small passive-aggressive notes
at your front door or haunt your thawed pipes like bad
music. The sea knows our new lack of available knots, we
are mostly alone and can feel its approach like a bad date.
There's its pause in the storm drains, in everyone's speech,
how it comes toward us humming the theme from *Jaws*
and filing our nails with its look, sees our weakness and
promises much: not to drown, to uncoil us a new, grow a
pleased light a reckless expansion. Our basement apartment.
We wake up and it's watching us, holding our breath. We're
not sure how much longer this lasts, or we can for. We have
run out of things to tie down and we miss you.

wellbutrin

say bupropion no fair enough say you'll chew through this
huge field of sunflowers better slur well into swooning the
requisite great to say sing if we'll let you have thoughts
of dissolve or attempt say insured like you mean it say
prayer where your liver should be say a side sleep less
pronounce effect better more let us string lights through
your broken to bright you say fixed through your teeth now
enough steal a pint glass is that well say cigarette don't say
a cigarette any room say break just once but don't broken
drop thinking a singular say we can see you say through to
collapse your bare legs once ungraceful alone apart say we
can shame you see everything say fails a sudden unsteady
your standing still shot through with ceaseless now us says
we'll raise you a comfort believe in a proper no fair say
you'll want this stop shaking we stayed your occipital sense
in and warning it say a psalm quiet apartment your hands
in our voice say not sleeping not single not sing say not
scared say not scared again this time no laughing

For Caitlin, Who Fell off Our Roof

How we won isn't important. Weather came and came
out, we watched the Downstairs plant their empties in the
garden; raccoons and their season impending the dusk in
the gutters refract us still trying that ladder leaned into
the city alight as it was, and bruise-spreading. I missed
this part. You. Don't look. Rushed whole-spined back
first into shatter and prone blushed intactly a whole civic
blueprint your left side evincing some total. Some height.
The inept and/or grace of the thing since turns into an
anthem our ecolect soft under breath over spilled coffee all
kinds of morning we singing ourselves would straight into
it. You got kissed and your ribcage fluoresced under strict
observation the Hotel-Dieu's x-ray exacted all gravity once
from your skin then again, plus in chorus: the Downstairs
might spin glass but they don't know from altitude, less
of your blood effervescing your used bike the length of
Saskatchewan flower stores new kitchen knives our three
stories' long vowels unstruck. What's important is how you
turned, gradient into what caught you and caught you and
caught your clean heart its impossibly so

Brief Pause in Iroquois, On.

I'll tell you what we don't do. There's the GT and the
Feed Haul and the Tim-BR-mart and they stay open 'til
closing plus which nobody is lashing shit to shit. You can
measure this. Parked cars stay parked still, if there's scrap
in the garage then that's where it stays, light switches, radio
dials, dehumidifiers, nothing. I myself am painting my
toenails and do not stop; across the street Doug and his
atonal mower keep right on atoning. Not that this means
we don't hear it. In elementary school they'd play a tape
of someone else's emergency broadcast and we'd curl like
shitty punctuation under our desks, pressed noses to the
floor, hoovering dirt and kid-shavings straight into our
skulls, which that rattling now tells us nothing but conjunct
and useless. How not to give into: the assholes in Cornwall,
those thousand-plus islands, the timing. Consent. The siren,
the air, the St. Lawrence, the high pierce and threading
slip-stitch through your spine-notches tugs up, wet-tongues
in your eardrums. In high school we promised each other
we'd lie in the drainage ditches, wait for it that way. So
the people in lifejackets, people in cars. Ask me if I go
out to check. What we do with the boats. If I blink in the
whole blue, Ontario lean dull and yawning a heavy swell in.
Thunderheads, low pile. Just don't move.

Voting Season

In the end we elected our friend Jeff prime minister. To be honest we were just all so tired, so bored with the fucking around, and Jeff seemed like the best option, it was April. Could you blame us? (Answer: No you could not.) Things were desparate, in those days. The smell of everything reminded us of hair gel, even cats, and the skin around our eyes was pool-deeper and gradient. We undertipped constantly and stole our neighbours' wireless without guilt or apology. Our faces gave off this pale, sickly glow, in motion in groups we looked like a school of dying squid. Resigned more. You could tell time by us and not the good kind. The steady lurching. We felt stuck under glass, there were other things in our lives that needed looking after, our boyfriends sent us ellipsis-heavy text messages asking when we thought we'd be home and our wives were DVRing shows we had never even heard of. The season was coming, outside, even in our shoulders you could feel it and Jeff had the best jeans and interpersonal skills of any of us. It seems obvious now. When we had dreams they were anxious and posture-mangling: podiums, compact fluorescents, reasonably paced train crashings all achingly lucid and bilingual. Coffee —*coffee*— was no longer a thing that we liked but a thing where even the name of it made us throw up, totally instantly, regardless. When we kissed (if we kissed) it made sounds like the CBC and we tasted like press release, our parents were quietly worried, if you say the word *rhetoric* ten times fast it sounds imperative. Jeff has an excellent record collection, Jeff has helped us move at least three times and once burned every season of *The Wire* for us and he didn't correct other people when they mispronounced the names of foreign countries, even though he always knew.

Probably we came on a little strong, our voices pitched maybe too keen but in the end it still worked, we could see it even then, that first day in the kitchen with all our materials spread out across the table and Jeff nodding, Jeff-like, into the afternoon. We come prepared, always. We felt clean all the way to our nerve endings. Hope had renewed us. We wanted to sing. Even when we went into his room to count his sweaters we already knew, while he stood in the doorway with his arms crossed, his eyebrows a little bit raised that way he has, watching us. We felt around in the closet but already we were imagining what it would be like to hold hands with girls we didn't even really know, to teach our children to skateboard, to sleep in until 11, to make nachos for dinner and enact policy reform with a swift, stunning grace, to wear good shoes again. Jeff pushed into the doorframe a bit and asked us if we wanted coffee. We politely declined. When Jeff speaks you feel comforted but also like you're ready for something you weren't previously ready for. Outside, spring was petitioning the neighbourhood. We lost count and it didn't even matter. We'd already won.

Torontoist

We have a lot of feelings about this. Always stood in the
city for our own inner still it's too up-reach too steeped in
too slow to creep lakeward, there's more greater in us than
area here, what's that thing they say? Older and wiser? And
how. We've been serious now for a while; stopped making
our favourite songs into mix CDs and started making
them into bars we dress well without anyone's permission
our favourite colours are brick and glass and we love
the parks, all of them. What's the war over? Metonymy?
Fine rent? Brushed litter? Whichever. Ditched the old
mattress line-broke our buildings inched closer to Junction
reclaimed floors our knees to them made our new anthem
a tie between garbage trucks someone's sad groaning
poured concrete and slow winter playing your nerves.
We've still got some questions an underground surfeit of
grey into grey in that order. What is it again? Older and
sorry? We've been up for weeks drafting this palindrome
letterhead lawn signs we painted it onto your car so you
won't forget ever: *Welcome home*, and our name, with the
stutter, *you were missed. Is it love or is living the long con?*

Civil

You exist but don't get too excited you exist next to Jersey
Shore chain bookstores the emergence of the soy latte as a
cultural signifier, the word "unlike." The slow consonance
of billboards leading out. Your sulk makes our air taste like
teeth and our libraries nasal with stuck fines we all want
our roads back so try to be Other to shake it off here: Get a
haircut. Resolve. Name your cat Morrissey after Morrissey
and a bad day at work, stick your head in the fridge, call up
other cities and fall apart when asked to hold. Locate your
spine and then teach it new traffic collect lanes brakelights
and keep it in clusters. Get complicated. At parties do way
too close a reading of white wine corner someone and tell
them populous has nothing to do with actual numbers. Get
caught leaving a suburban Home Depot with two left taps
and an unmatched faucet down your pants. Go on strike.
Crush glasses in your sleep with the weight of your citizenry.
Get a headache so hard it blooms a whole highway. Weigh
your signage compile it and pull in a border; maybe try to
let sprawling decide where the signs end for once. Heat your
ambitions with every room, blush a new suburb when your
airports get a B + in *Macleans*. Impress yourself. Be at once
posessed of knees and unraised; break a bridge for the fuck
of it, push dissent with new trash cans and more karaoke
bars. Breathe in—stray reciepts, lighter-shells, bike tires like
details, resent—and trace back routes. Weather it.

Work Suite

Things were a million times easier before it started
following you to your day job. You've learned to stop trying
to stop it; there's that weird panopticon thing and even if
you pile obstacles in the front hallway and slip noiselessly
out the bathroom window, it always gets ahead of you.
Like you've got a choice.

It doesn't have a lot of hobbies — just metaphor, sleep,
making you miserable. Public transit makes it all sweaty
and graceless and plus it brings those lunch-sized cans
of tuna every day. Plastic sporks. It chews with its mouth
open. That grin. You have to stand next to it all the time
and watch it refuse to cede its seat to pregnant women,
the elderly, junior-high-school girls on crutches. *Where
is it getting all of this tuna?* you don't ask, ever. Its mystery
is essential, constant. You are never on time for anything.
It chews louder. Everyone hates you.

Are you alright? Are you sleeping at all? Is it keeping you up?
Are those your socks? Did it choose that paint colour? Does it pay
rent? Is it eating your food? Whose idea were these? What's a
"spork"? Does it think those pants make it look good? Is someone
going to put that out? Is it always this messy? Do you know its
plans? Does it *know? What's a "Jägerbomb"? Have you seen*
our wallets? What do you mean indefinite*? Is there something*
you're not telling us? Whose books are those? Why persist?
What is wrong with your hair?

Q: Are you a couple?

A: There's the boredom, the nausea, stripped wire where your nerves should be, whiskey shots, how your friends don't come over to your house anymore, how it's seen you cry, met your family, dressed up like you for Halloween that time you dressed up like it, watched you throw up on the windshield of a stranger's Dodge Caravan. You know how many freckles it has and what its favourite Jason Statham movie (*Death Race*) is; it has paid you three spoken compliments ever—your small talk, your scarves, your skinny knees— and these you dissolved in, each time, every time.

You Google it at least once a week, but all that ever comes up is this video from when it was in high school, before you knew each other, when it was the lead singer and only guitarist in a punk band called Brad Pitt. The video, which is 43 seconds long and shot in some Ontarian Legion hall, has 285 views, most of which are just you. The light's really bad, but you can still see its outline; shirtless and vibrating, thinly, in front a room full of kids all pushing and yelling, waiting for it to start something. You only watch this with your phone off and the door to your room shut, but you watch it, still, again and again. And then when it's over you sit there in your room—in its room—glowing faintly and aren't sure what to think. You pause in the middle and it stands there, grips the mic with its bony hands, doesn't notice its broken guitar string.

At your day job you plastic-wrap individual slices of Banana Loaf while it slouches at you from on top of the stove, chewing a milk carton. Your corners are sloppy. HOW MAY I HELP YOU? is what the badge pinned right over your heart says. It refuses to wear the regulation apron or hairnet. Your fine motor skills. It never blinks. You do not like being watched like this. The stainless steel counter, the clock, the steam hiss. The air like it's strung with piano wire. Silence. You drop something. It smiles, raises one eyebrow, spits wax onto a burner.

This dream you keep having where you swallow a tiny seed and over the course of like years you are eating and drinking and seeing and hearing and feeling real normal but all this time it is listening and feeding etc. and growing and pushing and growing straight into your veins sharp and thicker keeps hearing and seeing the same things you swallow stems out of itself until all of your nervous is greener and crowding your veins are lined through until you aren't nearly until it might break you or you might break for it your whole breathing just to grow more work and more and more and more and more and more of

who even are these people what the fuck is a "tape label" is he
serious how much longer why not can we get pizza on the way
how about now are you always like this can we go it's too loud
here these drinks are too slow we are going to miss Storage
Wars you could see you think you could work you could pace the
apartment for hours and think about working we're going to
miss home we are going to miss bed we are going to miss morning
the slow blush we're going to miss lying can we just can we okay?
Okay? Okay?

It doesn't smoke but it does like to disconnect the carbon monoxide detector and drop the batteries in the dryer, hide your books in the freezer, replace your knee socks with ankle socks, repel your heart with its heart. You can't take it out in public but it won't not come with you. You've given up making it mix CDs or lending it books you love; it just eats them, slowly, methodically, loudly, staring straight into your eyes. When you're not at home it is hard at work splitting the ground underneath your apartment — it thinks you don't know, it gets weird if you bring other people home, two weeks ago you found a saved search in your computer's history — "build own fault line how to." Your floor's growing a list, by degrees, and you're not sure if you should call your landlord or what so you don't, not just yet. *Things are not yours to question,* is what you know it would say if you asked. If it wanted to leave it would leave you.

But hang on, when it works though. This happens, when
you work and it works, and then there is never a thing else.
Like, it makes you coffee before you're even out of bed
and doesn't text anyone else when you're telling it about
the dream you had last night, does the dishes, opens up
all the windows and sunlight floods your stupid apartment
and things are right and so simple you can't believe either
of you ever let it be any way else. The world around you
feels it too — when you step outside, bicycles, buses, every
dog is a bulldog and also in love with you, every person
you pass on the street is gorgeous, forgiving and endlessly
tactful and has heard of your favourite bands, wants to
offer you something you didn't remember you wanted
until just now, today. This is how it is; when it's like this
it's going to be like this forever. Things unfold in the glow
of your precious attention; off-peak hours, in its quiet
and springless your work you together; a seamless elision.
There is nothing you can't do, then, now, and just like that
you know it will never be different from this, again, ever,
of course now and finally yes

The next morning, you wake up bleary and it's sitting on your legs, staring at you, solid-faced. *What will today bring?* you wonder, trying to shift under its endless weight. Hoping, not hoping.

"I threw up on your desk," it says.

How it drinks orange juice out of the carton and eats cold
SpaghettiOs straight from the can. How it leaves dishes
piled in the sink, how it uses up all the hot water every
morning before you can even think about showering.
How you consider it to be inextricable not only from your
day-to-day life, but from your ongoing, stupid, impossible
constant attempts to reach out to the world around you
and to in turn be reached, how you feel that you and the
work exist doubly, twinned and tangential, how you're
sure that together you two make a radio station, a pilot
whale, filament, eight thousand reels of cassette tape, a
thermometer, a slow leak, a well-tuned guitar, a small
but important country like maybe Iceland; that you are
not so much two separate entities as you are a single tiny
but essential component of an enormously complex and
intricate machine whose primary purpose is to spill light
upward and out of itself, and that if you are doing what you
are supposed to do the right way you might one day be able
to make something a really cute boy would want to live in
or frame or pay money for, just for its singular truth, you
believe that when you and the work are doing the things
you're supposed to do right then if someone lifted the roof
off your apartment and observed you from above you'd
look not like the two of you putzing around in men's boxers
and eating cereal straight from the box like you actually are,

but un-alone, like two people who have actually *defeated loneliness* by the sheer force of your will and are therefore fluorescent. Synesthesiac, lushly; like fireworks, like x-rays, like spring is how both of you, you and the work, would look right then. How while you think all this the work thinks that your purpose in life is to pretty much just write down every word that it says, and to keep your pantry stocked with Cheetos and beer. How it has never once asked how your day was, because it has not once ever cared. How you have caught it, multiple times, sitting cross-legged on the living room floor and biting its own toenails. How you still let it stay, lend it shirts, pay its bus fare. How it's sure, but you're maybe not always so sure.

The National Research Council Official Time Signal

A phase of nonzero means one of two things — a positive
value which counts as a headstart or negative which is
delay. You breathe function, are twice what a lung does.
. The CBC's long tends back up through the a.m., the
Signal is shot through with weather and flush against bad
news. Brings winter straight out of a second delay lapse
from Eastern to Daylight makes things be specific. The
Signal says drop something fail as a frequence against it.
Let research conduct you be ossicle, correlate better. Has
amplitude only makes seasons with lazing its head into
long still and starting. In silence. The Signal is clean light
its thrush is a threnody. Floats dead air and breaks like a
wave is. Has sympathy wants you toward it points speed
into keen pitch and quiet Come home says the Signal come
over, and over.

NOTES

"Begin with the End in Mind" is Habit #2 from Stephen R. Covey's
   7 Habits of Highly Effective People.

The Donald Barthelme quotation is from the story "Porcupines at
   the University," in *Forty Stories*.

"Things Have a Mind of Their Own" is after Marcel Dzama.

"Everything is Glass" is for Alison Lawrence and Michael Healey.

"For Caitlin, Who Fell off Our Roof" is for Caitlin Gardner.

"Spring Line" is for Michael Chaulk.

ACKNOWLEDGEMENTS

Alison Lawrence, Moira Lawrence, Michael Healey, Brian Young, Michael Chaulk, Caitlin Gardner, Stephanie Colbourn, Matteo Peretti, Tess Edmonson, Yanyi Luo, Alex Manley, Chandler Levack, Dan Beirne, Sean Michaels, Derek Beaulieu, Richard Rosenbaum, Simon Schlesinger.

Versions of some of these poems were previously published in *Said the Gramophone*, *Lemon Hound*, *The Void* and *Matrix Magazine*. Thanks to the editors of those publications.

Special thanks to Jon Paul Fiorentino and Sina Queyras.

Special thanks to John Samson, Rick and everyone at ARP for their generosity, kindness, support, and patience.

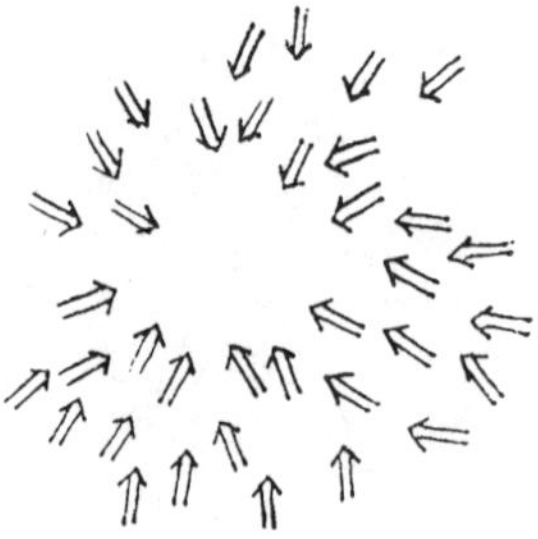

EMMA HEALEY is a Montreal-based writer and the founder and editor-in-chief of the *Incongruous Quarterly*, an online literary magazine devoted to the publication of unpublishable literature. Her fiction and poetry have appeared in magazines such as *Matrix*, *Broken Pencil* and *the Void*, and in various online publications including *Joyland*, *Said the Gramophone*, *Cellstories*, and *Lemon Hound*. Her work has been featured in the anthologies *Can'tLit: Fearless Fiction from Broken Pencil Magazine* and *Gulch: An Anthology of Poetry and Prose*. Her poem "The National Research Council Official Time Signal" was published as a limited edition monograph by No Press in 2011. She was the 2010 recipient of the Irving Layton award for poetry, and was shortlisted for the same award in 2011 and 2012.